15

D0315788

Based on the episode "Paddington's First Halloween" by Toby Davies

Adapted by Lauren Holowaty

First published in Great Britain by
HarperCollins *Children's Books* in 2020
HarperCollins *Children's Books* is a division of HarperCollins*Publishers* Ltd,
HarperCollins Publishers
1 London Bridge Street
London SE1 9GF

The HarperCollins website address is:
www.harpercollins.co.uk

1 3 5 7 9 10 8 6 4 2

ISBN: 978–0–00–836800–5

Printed in China

Based on the Paddington novels written and created by Michael Bond

PADDINGTON™ and PADDINGTON BEAR™ © Paddington and Company/STUDIOCANAL S.A.S. 2020
Paddington Bear™ and Paddington™ and PB™ are trademarks of Paddington and Company Limited
Licensed on behalf of STUDIOCANAL S.A.S. by Copyrights Group

MIX
Paper from
responsible sources

FSC
www.fsc.org   FSC® C007454

FSC is a non-profit international organisation established to promote the
responsible management of the world's forests. Products carrying the FSC
label are independently certified to assure consumers that they come
from forests that are managed to meet the social, economic and
ecological needs of present and future generations.

Find out more about HarperCollins and the environment at
www.harpercollins.co.uk/green

The Adventures of Paddington™

First Halloween

HarperCollins *Children's Books*

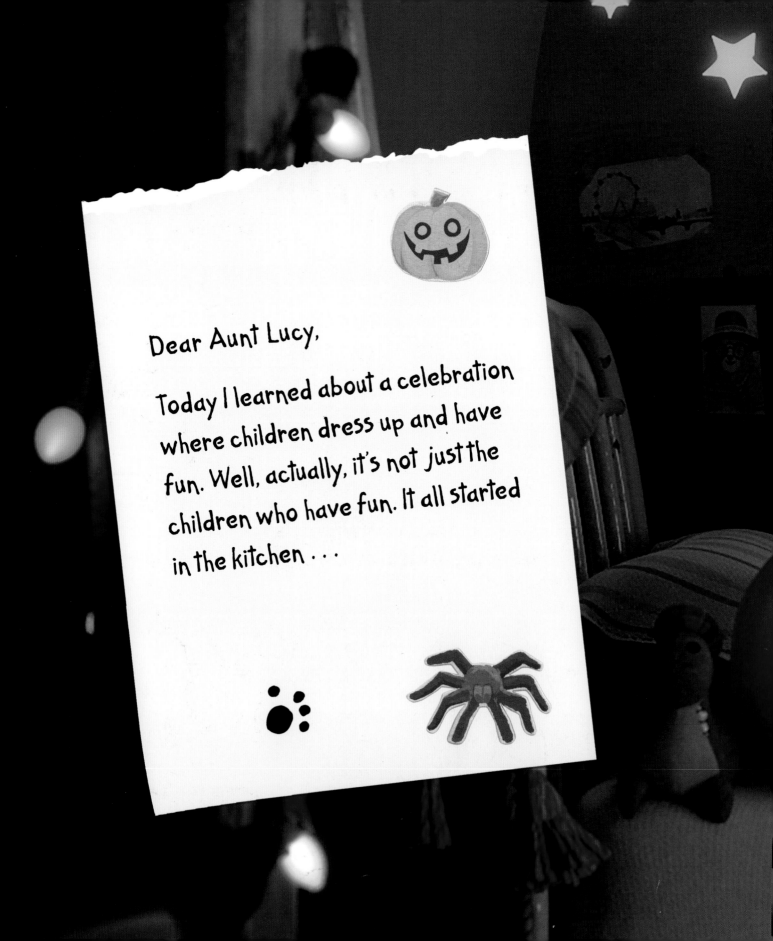

Dear Aunt Lucy,

Today I learned about a celebration where children dress up and have fun. Well, actually, it's not just the children who have fun. It all started in the kitchen . . .

The Browns were looking at a pile of **strange decorations** on the kitchen table.

"It's Halloween," said Mrs Brown, "a special day when people dress up and do things to scare beasties away."

"That *doesn't* sound fun . . ." said Paddington.

"Oh, it is!" said Jonathan.

"We'll show you!"

Paddington helped Judy and Mrs Bird put up Halloween decorations on the outside of the house. There were ghosts, spiders, cobwebs and pumpkins everywhere.

"This doesn't seem all that scary," said Paddington, feeling relieved.

Suddenly, a bouncy bat decoration swooped
down towards Paddington, making him jump!

"ARGHHH!"

"Sorry!" Jonathan
shouted from the balcony
above them.

"Why don't you join us, Mr Curry?" asked Paddington politely when the Browns' neighbour arrived home. "We're having all sorts of Halloween fun."

"No, thank you. I *hate* Halloween," Mr Curry grumbled. "I shall lock my door, turn my lights off and be glad when it's all over."

. . . Paddington **toppled** out of the treehouse! Luckily, he managed to grab hold of a rope, and sail safely down to the ground.

But the pumpkin came tumbling down after Paddington, and landed right on his head! SQUELCH!

"I'm OK!" he mumbled from inside the pumpkin, wobbling from paw to paw.

Mrs Bird had told Mr Brown that nothing would scare her, so he sneaked up on her while she was doing the washing-up.

"Raaaar!"

But she didn't even blink.

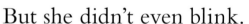

He hid in the bathroom cupboard to frighten her when she opened the door, but she piled toilet rolls on top of him and calmly walked away.

BOING!

He even gave her a trick box of nuts
to open, with a springy snake
hidden inside. But nothing happened . . .

. . . until he
opened it himself.

"AHHHH!"

Meanwhile, Jonathan and Judy helped Paddington get ready.

"Tell me again," asked a puzzled Paddington, "why am I dressed as Pigeonton?"

Jonathan explained that on Halloween people dress up and go trick-or-treating. "If people don't give us a treat, we play a trick."

Paddington thought that sounded a little mean. "Would
you mind awfully if I do '*treat*-or-treat' instead?"

"Treat-or-treating? That *does* sound much nicer,"
agreed Mrs Brown as they set off. "Let's try it!"

When they arrived at Mr Gruber's shop, he made them **jump** by popping out of a **huge pumpkin!**

"Treat or treat?" Paddington asked, offering him a marmalade roll.

"Oh my goodness!" gasped a delighted Mr Gruber. "Thank you, and here are some treats for all of you."

"And here's a little treat for *you*!" said Paddington, offering him another marmalade roll.

"Happy Halloween, Mr Gruber!" everyone cheered as they waved goodbye.

"Happy *Noche de Brujas*!" cheered Sofia when the treat-or-treaters arrived at her café.

"Oh, dear," said Paddington, looking worried. "We aren't celebrating that, Sofia. We are celebrating Halloween."

"Don't worry," said Sofia, "*Noche de Brujas* is what we call
Halloween **in Columbia.** Here are some treats for you."
And she put sweets in all their buckets.

"Thank you, and here is *your* treat, Sofia," said Paddington,
kindly offering her a marmalade sandwich from his hat.

After a few more visits, the treat-or-treaters arrived home.

"Welcome back," said Mrs Bird. "Did you have a good time?"

"For the world's first treat-or-treat session," said Judy, holding out her full bucket, "I'd say it was brilliant!"

But Paddington had noticed something odd . . .

Mr Curry's door was open.

"That's strange," said Mrs Bird. "He said he was going to lock his door as he didn't like Halloween. I do hope he's all right."

Mr Brown thought they should check, so they all crept inside . . .

"Mr Curry! Are you all right?"
Mrs Bird called.

There was a rattle from underneath a metal dish on the kitchen table. Mrs Bird slowly picked it up and . . .

"Boo!" "ARGHHH!"

. . . she screamed when she saw **Mr Curry's head**
underneath, painted green and surrounded by sausages!

Mr Brown raced in laughing. "We flapped the unflappable Mrs Bird!"

"Best Halloween ever!" Mr Curry and Mr Brown said together, delighted that their trick had worked.

"You didn't scare me," replied Mrs Bird at first, and then changed her tune. "OK, you did!"

"But, Mr Curry, I thought you didn't like Halloween," said Paddington, feeling a bit confused. "I'm afraid I don't have any treats left."

"I love Halloween! I just pretended not to for Mr Brown's plan," explained Mr Curry. "Don't worry, bear, making Mrs Bird jump was *my* treat!"

We decided it was much more fun to give treats rather than tricks, apart from Mr Curry, who really liked the trick he and Mr Brown played on Mrs Bird. Really, they behaved just like children!

Happy Halloween!

Love from,

Paddington